LITTLE SCOOT

REBECCA KAI DOTLICH
ILLUSTRATED BY EDSON IKÊ

BOYDS MILLS PRESS

AN IMPRINT OF BOYDS MILLS & KANE

New York

Little Scoot shivers under cloudy skies
with seagulls and ships
in her tugboat eyes.

Dispatcher blares,
"Big Barge can't BUDGE.
Little Scoot, he's STUCK, go give him a nudge."

Little Scoot nods. "That's a job I can do!"
But oh, how she wishes the skies were clear blue.

And yet . . .

...the little tug puffs
and the little tug toots ...
then scoots.

Out on the sea a thunderstorm's brewing.
Little Scoot worries. "Oh, *what* am I doing?
This might be the stormiest storm I've been in."

And yet . . .

. . . she **TOOTS** and she puffs and
she squares up her chin.

Scoot sails ahead as the gusty storm grows.
Skies rumble and tumble.
A windy wind blows.

Waters go **SPLASH**.
Waters go **SPLOSH**.
Little Scoot sputters,
galoosh, galosh.

SLASH Splosh

She wants to turn back,
but there's **BIG** work to do,

SO ...

. . . she straightens her stack
and pushes right through.

Scoot squeezes her eyes
as she's tossed by a wave.
"This is scary," she mumbles,
"but I'm *trying* to be brave."

Waves whoosh in her eyes.
Waves swoosh in her mouth.
And yet . . .

. . . she straightens her stack as her compass points south.

But oh, how she wishes
the waves were glass blue,
as she hopes a true hope
that Barge comes into view.

And there,
    stuck and stranded . . .
    Big Barge sits!

    "I'm coming!" she toots,
        "Little Scoot never quits."

I'M COMING!

She pushes and pulls, but it isn't enough—
The waves are **SO** big.
The waves are **SO** rough.

She thinks hard, then spins
and straightens her stack,
with her lamps turned on,
with the wind at her back . . .

AND

with one mighty push

and one mighty pull

out of sand, out of muck . . .

...Big Barge is

UNSTUCK!

Little Scoot winks
and sighs a tug sigh.

Then she *chug, chug, chugs*

AND WHISTLES...

Now snug in her harbor,
the rain barely spits
as she toots a proud toot:
"Little Scoot never quits."

For London, my newest Little Scoot —RKD

*For all children; remember that
even in bad times, there will always be a
flame of light to help you overcome
the storms of life —EI*

Text copyright © 2021 by Rebecca Kai Dotlich / Illustrations copyright © 2021 by Edson Ikê
All rights reserved. Copying or digitizing this book for storage, display, or distribution in any other medium is strictly prohibited.

For information about permission to reproduce selections from this book, please contact permissions@bmkbooks.com.

Boyds Mills Press
An imprint of Boyds Mills & Kane, a division of Astra Publishing House
boydsmillspress.com
Printed in China

ISBN: 978-1-63592-300-1 (hc) / 978-1-63592-379-7 (eBook)
Library of Congress Control Number: 2019953786

First edition / 10 9 8 7 6 5 4 3 2 1

Design by Barbara Grzeslo / The text is set in Gill Sans Std. / The illustrations are digital.